THE UNBECOMING:
A JOURNEY
WITHIN

∞

RENEÉ R. MUDREY, PHD.

∞

For information regarding special discounts for bulk purchases, please contact Dr. Renee at 330-400-1000 or drrenee@transcendentheart.com

Manufactured in the United States of America but written with my soul in India

ISBN-13: 9781790320431

DEDICATION

∞

This book is dedicated to my Father who inspired me to read, write, create and go to the unimaginable places in my mind.

CONTENTS

∞

Shattered and slayen
In pain and in vain
But with faith held tight
Yearning to fly there she goes breaking chains

With wings made of fire and with beauty of her pain
The rocks piercing her feet or wild winds were to blame
Her breath was to life that rose as a flame
And a soul with a vessel with a beautiful brain

Brave are the souls that take a chance
To let loose the boundaries, shackles and chains
A journey, a flight, a life of light
Beginning to the Unbecoming..
As she stood in the rain.
G..

PROLOGUE

∞

*T*he Unbecoming: A Journey Within, is the first book in a three-book series. The book represents the soul path of Liv, a young precocious girl who finds herself amidst trauma and crisis over the course of her life. The first gateway to the soul is represented in her awakening after the death of her Father, Robert. She then is visited by five key guides who aid her journey through various dimensions of consciousness. Liv faces several battles to let go of the conditioning and dogma she has acquired within the 3D reality. These guides find her at various crises in her life such as the loss of her father, self-limiting and defeating beliefs, and her own battle with cancer. Liv travels through parallel planes of consciousness to begin her battle to unlearn and essentially "unbecome" all that has hindered her from seeing her true higher self. The journey is a cleansing of the soul for Liv in which the unmistakable quiet inner voice is unveiled to her. The book is a science fiction novel sure to keep you on your toes guessing what is next to come for dear Liv. The book ends in India, a pivotal turning point for Liv in releasing the chains of the 3D world, and a dramatic shift in identifying herself with her divine purpose. Liv moves into a state of allowing of true self love and transcendence of mind, body, and spirit.

Book two is the story of Liv and the Man and their journey throughout India. Just as Liv felt the release through the unbecoming, she now has to find balance in remaining within the nothingness. How does one not fall back into old habits, patterns, and ways? This will be the ultimate story of Liv as she adjusts to the purest form of just being. The story will highlight Liv's true acceptance of seeing the Universe as not outside of her but within her bones and her soul. You will also witness the resulting self-love story that emerges within India.

Book three is the culmination of the story, the ultimate evolution...the ascension of the soul. The story will showcase important questions such as what is a soul. What does every soul search for? Is ascension synonymous with enlightenment? Liv and the Man will fight their greatest battles to save humanity from itself and move into multi-dimensional being and beyond.

Introduction

And when you fall in love with all of thyself

mind body and soul, you will fall in love

with all of creation and become one.

Become whole.

Several years ago, I found myself with this underlying desire to write my life story. When you are a woman in her mid-forties, you have a lot to tell. There is a lot of baggage. There is a lot of hurt. There is a lot of triumph, but there is also a lot of tragedy. There is a lot of starting over and there are a lot of endings. There was so much to tell that this book would have been volumes by the time I was finished telling "my story." Many people go on and successfully write their life story in that way, but I knew I wanted to do something different. I am a Professor. I am used to writing journal articles, clinical reports, and things that are objective. I did not want to look at my life in an objective lens anymore. I desired to look at my life through something more colorful, something more vibrant. I wanted to heal and I wanted to help others heal as well.

I found myself wondering what was it in my life that kept me stuck in this karmic loop. Every time I would move forward, I would take two steps back. What was it? And then I had this "a-ha" moment. I realized that it wasn't that I needed to become anything anymore. In fact, I needed to "unbecome". I needed to let go. I needed to shed, to unravel, to release. I needed to set down everything that I thought was mine, but wasn't. You know, everything that is given to us out of goodness from other people, but we simply outgrow and realize it does not fit our lives anymore. Things that were truly belonging to other people and not myself. I needed to let that go, and I tried. Trust me...I tried. I tried in therapy for years, for decades actually. I tried in different types of coaching and I was successful to a point. I went to an entrepreneurial coach to learn how to start my business. I went to a spiritual coach to heal those parts of me and I did well, but there was still a piece missing.

The piece that was missing was the piece that I wasn't looking for at all. In fact, when I was a little girl, my favorite book was "The Missing Piece," by Shel Silverstein. I still read this book to my current students every semester. Some of my students are preparing to teach high school students, some even college students. They look at me like, "why are you reading this children's book to me"? But then the magic happens. As I read the story, I see their eyes light up with the "Oh my God, I get it" moment. This is every teacher's dream. We search in our lives for these missing pieces. We feel like we are a puzzle. We feel like we are always in lack. We feel like there is something more, or something else to gain. In fact, this is why we struggle. There is nothing else to gain. In fact, we had everything when we were born. That is why I love the second book in the series, "The Missing Piece Meets The Big O," by Shel Silverstein.

The missing piece meets this circle who is completely full in the entirety of itself. There is no room for this piece and the Big O tells it to go on, but the piece keeps trying to fit. It tries to squeeze in but it does not make it. Then it realizes that it just needs to become less to transform its' shape to start moving. It did not need to become a part of another or to even add any additional pieces to itself. It was everything all by itself. The missing piece, was truly not missing anything. It just had transformed what it already was. This is what "The Unbecoming" is all about. The "Unbecoming" is a process in which you come to this beautiful place of recognizing that you are enough. You are more than enough. You've always been enough, and through the goodness of probably many of your family members, friends, teachers, coworkers, colleagues, bosses, spiritual leaders, etc., whomever you sought help through, really did their best. However, many of these people simply were giving you what they lacked, what they yearned for, what they needed.

As a result, this book is a labor of love. It is a true journey of my own self as I have spent so much time picking pieces up, taking on other people's tragedies, and even absorbing people's pain. I also spent many years packing my own pain up and revisiting it like it was an award or a trophy or something that I needed to keep looking at. A dear soul in my life once asked me, "Why do you keep checking that box? Just check the box. Let it be." I didn't know how to be. I just knew how to go out and get it. I'm a girl who grew up in the 1980s and 1990s which was a beautiful time of contemporary feminism. Women could be anything and damn it, I tried. I was a successful school teacher. Later, I went on and earned a Ph.D. for God's sake. I grew up in the inner city and was born to parents who had no money, no education, and no cultural capital.

I made a lot of my life...too much some may argue. I was not wealthy by any means, but I had a lot of accomplishments and I tried to find the peace in my life through what I was doing and through whom I was with. The inner peace never came. Over the course of my life, I found myself in five key aspects, five key moments in which I was searching, searching, searching, when in actuality, I realized I had started my own "Unbecoming". I wasn't even aware of it. First, was the death of my Father. My Dad was my everything. He was my childhood hero, my childhood friend, my confidant, my teacher, my study partner. He was everything. When he died, I felt as though a part of me died and I went out searching to comfort that pain to fill that void.

The second aspect of my life was my relationship with my Mother. After my Dad passed, my Mom lost her way, as I'm sure it must not have been easy to lose your life partner after 41 years. I never truly felt a deep bond with my Mother growing up. She was busy. She was working. In her defense, she was trying to take care of us, just doing the best that she could and what she knew how to do. My Mother had a lot of traumas in her own life. I feel that I went on to struggle with my own belief in my ability to be a Mother due to the lacking bond I had with my own. I didn't trust myself as a woman, especially a divine mother who could bear and take care of children as they deserved. I would go on to struggle with fertility issues even when I did attempt to have children.

Similar to my Father, my Mother had a lot of wounding in her own life. I somehow picked up their wounding and decided I wanted to carry it forward for them. I did not make this choice consciously, but it is what I did. I went on to carry the wounding of two grown people like a backpack. Like a penance I had not asked for nor wished for. That is a pretty heavy load for a child to carry, but somehow I managed. For some reason I began to live out my parents wounding within my own reality. Their stories became my story and I started to find similar relationships and live out similar experiences. Thus, perpetuating a generational cycle of wounding.

The third aspect of my life that emerged, something I never saw coming, was my deep rooted fear that I would perish just as my father did. I was obsessed with my health and my anxiety went through the roof. I did not smoke, I took care of myself, and I really did things differently in my life. There was no reason for me to believe that his life would become my reality, but for some reason I did and I found myself with the self-fulfilling prophecy coming to life. Several years later I found myself getting that dreaded phone call of the diagnosis of cancer, melanoma cancer, in fact, and it was a scary time for me. It was one where I had to face my own

12

mortality in a way. I was in my early forties, I had two children who were both very young at the time. I just could not imagine them living their lives without me. I lived without my father at this point for several, several years, and the pain never went away. The pain is still with me today and I just couldn't even think of what life would be like for my Olivia, and my Aleks without their mother. And so that became a whirlwind for me. The pain with the surgery to reconstruct my leg, the pain of being told that I had other types of tumors growing in my body because of it, and the constant worry, constant fear that I would just die from cancer.

And then there was this moment when everything fell apart in my life. My husband had turned away, wanted nothing to do with me. I felt lost. I felt rejected. I felt abandoned at everything I thought I had in my life. One thing after another just sort of walked away and left me or let me down. I remember feeling this huge uneasiness about not being able to look in the mirror anymore at my body and myself. I did not like what I was looking at. It was like I was facing this war with the monsters of chronic shame, guilt and hurt. I just simply lost all love of self. I don't think I ever truly loved myself. Whatever I had, I lost. I started to have financial hardship and just one problem after the other kept emerging. Then I found myself thinking it would be better to leave this planet. But for some reason, as my beautiful friend, Amberly Lago has been quoted saying, I was so petrified to live, but I was more afraid to die. I looked up to the sky and begged the angels that something had to shift for me. Something had to change. Just in that moment, a beautiful warm light came over my face. It was warm and comforting. It was the most beautiful light one could ever imagine. The interesting point here is that it was already dark outside. Yet with this light, I felt a deep embrace on my hand as to tell me all was taken care of. All would be ok. The next several years were just that...ok enough to cope and get by.

Just a year ago, I found myself traveling to India. India was a place I had never been. In fact, I had never been on a plane that long by myself. Yet, I found myself taking a chance on love and on myself for the first time. I was braving uncertainty and the anxiety had seemed to lessen. I was off to meet my spiritual teacher, my best friend whom I had grown very close to over that year. I landed in India only to have the most amazing feeling wash over me once again. This warm, bright light shined over me. Yet again, I was in the dark. I felt

14

like I had been here a million times before. I felt like I was truly home.

I had somehow come to a sense of divine knowing, divine purpose, and found a place of peace while traveling in India. I found myself looking in the eyes of someone whom I had waited for my entire life. My father had told me stories of this man that I would meet, told me to hold on, told me to have faith. He told me that a heart like yours, "Blue" (my childhood nickname), could only be loved by someone like you. My father told me to trust that this soul was out there. Indeed he was. I found myself staring in the eyes of myself. The ultimate mirror. The ultimate reflection. The one who was never going to let me fall apart again.

I was staring at the most beautiful aspect of myself I ever could have asked for, my divine masculine, challenging me to stay and embrace my divine feminine. This was the very aspect that I had always looked away from my whole life. In fact, I had always stepped into the divine masculine role. It felt more comfortable. It just felt fitting. It felt safe. Every time I tried to release, let go, be in my divine feminine energy, I was overwhelmed with fear. I just couldn't do it. And this beautiful soul standing before me holding my hand, looking into my eyes had reminded me, he too, had been waiting for me. He was taking care of our roots, our soul, while I was taking care of the branches up above.

I realized that in that moment, all that I thought I had or I ever thought I was, had nothing to do with what I was at that very moment. The true essence of my soul had been revealed. As a result, I am writing this book to the unbecoming for you because I wish I had this decades ago. I wish I had heard someone tell me you don't have to be anything more. Now you can go on and you can be whatever you want in your career. You can go on and have as many children as you like and go on and be married or choose not to be married. You can own businesses, you can stay home to raise your children. You can just live a life by yourself, wandering the planet. You can do whatever you wish. Inner peace will not come through acquiring things or looking for that one to save you. It is about coming to a space of knowing your true value in what you are in your barest, ultimate, truest form. This book will guide you along your own unbecoming.

Within this book you will find the synchronicity of 555. Five chapters, five key aspects of my life, and the five key guides who were there guiding me through every moment.

You will read about the significance of my own healing, happiness, and life satisfaction as it came through learning how to surrender, release, and ultimately find my way back to me. The "true" me. I certainly spent enough of my life fighting, struggling, or engaged in a relentless pursuit of what I thought I wanted for me. Now is the time to share with you, the readers, a story of unbecoming, or releasing all we thought we were to be, and essentially shedding it all to reclaim our divine essence from birth. We were perfectly created with a divine purpose. We simply thought we lost our way.

Within *The Unbecoming*, you will meet Liv, a young woman who awakens after the loss of her father only to find that she does not even recognize the woman staring back at her each day in the mirror. She questions who she is becoming and struggles to find her way through life. Liv is met throughout the story by five key guides who essentially show her the way to self-actualization, however, it doesn't come as she imagined. The number 5 represents freedom, exploration, travel, change and spiritual journey for Liv. Change is definitely on the horizon for Liv as she makes the ultimate sacrifice for self-discovery and transcendence, unlearning, surrendering, and letting go. The ultimate journey to the Unbecoming.

In Chapter 1, the beautiful relationship of Liv and her Dad, Robert is revealed. Liv's Dad is the one true soul who understands Liv, despite her anxiety and social phobias. You will also meet the Wise Old Oak who is a magical tree under which Liv and her Dad spent many days and nights. However, it is through these special moments that Liv has with the Wise Old Oak which truly shape her future. Liv and her Dad also spend many lived experiences together under the stars always yearning to learn more. Liv truly develops her love of knowledge through her Dad. You will fall in love with this divine pair as they conquer their own fears and limitations together. Liv's Dad will face his ultimate life battle which will bring these two to a spiritual plane never imagined.

Within Chapter 2, Liv is struggling to find her footing in the 3D reality, doubting the power of love, positivity, and hope. Instead, she finds herself buried deep within pain, anguish, and despair. She faces her darkest moment contemplating continuing in her journey and in this life. The pain is almost too unbearable. She is met by a divine guide, Lucina, the Goddess of Light, who illuminates the need for Liv to keep going and presents her with two very special gifts which will help Liv throughout her next few journeys.

Chapter 3 is representative of the inner battle Liv faces in her own identification with her divine feminine. Her struggling relationship with her Mother, and fears of becoming a Mother herself are highlighted in this part of the book as she finds herself in Iceland. Iceland is the homeland of her Mother, Anna, but she not only finds herself in her Mother's land, but is faced with the demons of her Mother as a young girl. Liv will have to make a decision between honoring her Mother and surrendering her need to fight the pain. A special gift from Lucina will play a significant role in this chapter and highlight the power of the divine feminine.

Chapter 4 is the scene of the quintessential battle Liv faces to truly "unbecome". She is defeated initially in the battle and has to go within to truly be one with her higher self. She is fearful to identify with her divine power, but has the amazing Destroyer as a guide to push her to the depths of lifting the veil of limiting self-beliefs and fears once and for all. How will she come to terms with a life threatening situation?

Chapter 5 finds Liv in India. She is faced with the loss of her childhood friend and confidant, the Wise Old Oak. It is the pivotal turning point in Liv's understanding of creation and her own divine power as the Mother of All. Liv finds herself face to face with the Man her Dad promised would find her. What will happen next for Liv and the Man? The gift from Lucina certainly becomes even more intriguing within this chapter. Trust, you will not want to miss a step in this exciting tale. Now sit back and enjoy a journey into *The Unbecoming.*

Chapter 1

Daddy's Girl

∞

Is it really so that the one I love is everywhere?

-Rumi

Liv was a precocious little girl. Eyes of sapphire blue, strawberry-blonde hair, and skinny as a rail. She was known to many as brilliant, but demanding. Liv always lived in her own world, one in which she created the most beautiful reality for herself and others. Liv needed this alternate reality as she often suffered from severe panic attacks, anxiety, and social phobias. Needless to say, Liv was not an average little girl by any means to others, even Liv's mother found her to be quite difficult. Liv often questioned the reality of God, the Universe, and all the unexplainable things most adults never talked about.

Liv was loved by her teachers but had few friends. It was difficult for Liv to connect with others as she often experienced immense nervousness in crowds and with those she was unfamiliar. In fact, Liv's first day of Kindergarten was not the typical fun day spent singing and dancing in a circle, but instead was met with the Catholic school Nun chasing her out of the bathroom where she was hiding in sheer panic. Despite Liv's advanced intellectual abilities and creative mind, teachers often wanted to hold her back fearing her lacking social skills would hinder her later in life.

Liv was also bullied equally by boys and girls when she was little. She was even violently punched in the stomach by a girl twice her size. Liv never understood how other kids could be so mean but never retaliated. When her Mother asked about her day, Liv would often brush off the difficult moments and tell her Mother all was well. This was certainly not the case for Liv. But for some reason, she felt the need to hide her pain from her Mother. As time went on, making friends became a bit easier. Liv was accepted to a school for the gifted in the third grade and she commented that she felt she was finally with kids who were just as 'weird' as she was. At this new school, the teachers never mentioned Liv's social limitations to her parents, and instead found many positons of leadership and academics in which Liv shined. It seemed she had truly found her home away from home. Despite Liv's social awkwardness, she had a best friend she could just be herself with and who she loved deeply. Liv's best friend was her Dad, Robert.

Robert was a scholar but never spent a day in school past eleventh grade. He was a hard working blue-collar man, but loved all things history and culture and spoke just as much as Liv despite being dyslexic and also suffering social anxiety. Together, they were inseparable, and they both had a tremendous love for learning. They were quite the pair. Liv's Dad would read mountains of books to her each week and Liv would do the same for her Dad. Liv's favorite book was *Dr. Doolittle*. Her Dad would imitate the various voices of the animals and make the book come alive. Every night during the work week, Liv would sit in her bedroom waiting for her Dad to arrive home from his second shift job. She could see just enough outside her window to catch the headlights of her father's car coming down their street.

While she waited excitedly for her Dad to arrive, Liv would often talk to the oak tree that sit right outside her bedroom window. She and her Dad named this tree, the Wise Old Oak. Liv's Dad said that she could talk to the Wise Old Oak any time she missed him while he was away at work or anytime they were not together. The Wise Old Oak had a branch that reached close to the house. It was as if you could reach out and touch its hand. For some reason Liv's Dad never trimmed this branch seeing this as more of a special trait about the tree. However, Liv never touched the tree other than to sit underneath and admire its majestic presence. She remembered reading *The Giving Tree* with her father and always worried about harming the Wise Old Oak. She revered the tree and its divinity in her life. Liv had many conversations with the Wise Old Oak often telling him all about her fears, wishes and dreams. To Liv, the wise tree seemed to accept her for who and what she was and listened to her with loving ears. Many nights they would both appreciate the various phases of the Moon in the night sky. The New Moon was Liv's favorite as she remembered learning about how it was the time when the Sun and the Moon were quite close to each other in the sky. Liv would imagine it as when they were close enough to hold hands. Liv also loved star gazing with the Wise Old Oak. The celestial wonder of Orion was their favorite.

During the summer months, Liv's Dad would read her many stories under the tree including several about the

Hunter, Orion. Liv's Dad told her all about the prominent constellation and that no matter where one may be in the world, this was one of the most recognizable and visible. "Just like the Moon, Daddy?" asked Liv. "Yes, my dear, just like the Moon. You can look up into the sky and talk to the Moon or Orion and messages will be sent clear across the planet." Liv's Dad talked about another constellation in the sky, Cassiopeia, commenting how it looked like an angel looking down upon them. Despite having few friends, Liv never felt lonely as she was the luckiest little girl in the world having so many guardians and angels watching over her every move. It was like the entire Universe always had eyes on Liv. Liv's Dad would talk about how brave Liv was and how she was the most beautiful Goddess in the Universe. Liv's Dad would talk for hours about how the Goddesses never wavered in their purpose and path despite fear and uncertainty. There were many Gods and Goddesses from Norse mythology that Liv loved learning about, including Freya. Liv's Mother often mentioned that Liv reminded her of Freya because of her bravery and golden heart. This special time with her Dad was definitely one of the moments she would always remember.

As Liv would spend time under the stars with Wise Old Oak, she would await the roar of her Dad's car, like a bat signal to Liv's tiny ears, and she knew her Dad was home. Every night, exactly at 12:15 a.m., Liv's Dad would turn into the driveway from work. Liv's Dad was never a second late. Liv would quietly sneak out of her bedroom so as to not awaken her Mother. Liv was quite gifted at escaping from her bedroom to spend this special time with her Dad. The two would watch TV for hours on end and talk all about their daily adventures at school and work. Many conversations happened in these late hours including the most special time Liv could recall well into her adult years.

Liv was seven at the time, curled up on her Dad's lap having a blissful time with her hero when she asked her Dad if he would always love her. "Of course", he replied, "but know one thing my dear. There will be someone in your future who will love you even more than I do." Of course Liv was stunned. She became quite sad actually, grabbing her Dad's hand tightly, and replied, "no one can love me more than you, Daddy." Liv's Dad lovingly replied, "Oh my love, one should love you more than me, and this will be the one who will bear his soul to you. This will be your love. Go and ask the Wise Old Oak and see what he says. I bet he will agree with me." Liv's Dad kissed her on her forehead and smiled knowing she would have a clever come back as she always did.

In fact Liv replied, "Ewwwww Daddy, boys are gross, and I simply have no need for their foolishness." As Liv was at that age and wanted nothing to do with boys so it was easy to see her Dad as the greatest love ever. Liv's Dad chuckled with his infamous belly laugh and reminded Liv she will change her mind someday and that even strong-willed Goddesses fall in love. Liv's Dad went on to describe the love he is referring as the "special one" who will understand her divine spirit. After reading her favorite book, Liv's Dad gave her a kiss goodnight on her forehead, tucked her gently into bed, and wished his princess off to sweet dreams. These secret late night meetings with Dad went on for several years into Liv's teen years. The two always had a special bond. Liv's Dad even became her study buddy throughout high school and her undergraduate days. Liv's Dad had the pleasure of seeing Liv graduate high school with the distinguished honor of being Valedictorian of her high school class. Even when college became more difficult than high school ever was, Liv's Dad would remind her that there was nothing she was not able to accomplish in her life and to keep positive no matter what. He was definitely the greatest cheerleader one could ever have.

The bond was so special that when Liv's Dad was diagnosed with lung cancer, a few years later, he knew she would be greatly impacted, possibly even more so than his other children. Liv's Dad knew he had to have a special conversation just with her. One day, after his chemotherapy treatment, Liv's Dad placed his hand on her shoulder while she was preparing dinner for her Dad. "Do you have a minute to talk?" asked her Dad. "Of course," replied Liv with a smile. Liv was now into her 20s. She had graduated summa cum laude, earned her Master's Degree and was just accepted into a doctoral program. Of course her Dad was extremely proud.

Knowing the connection these two always had since Liv was a little girl, Liv's Dad told her that he knew the cancer was spreading into his brain and that this would most likely impact his ability to talk or possibly alter his personality. Liv's Dad lovingly asked Liv to make a promise. "Sure, Daddy. What is it?" Liv's Dad looked directly into her blue eyes and said, "Baby, if I do anything or say anything in these next few weeks or months please know it isn't me. I will be nothing more than an empty vessel of a sick man. I know how important our conversations have been over our time together and I don't want these to stop, but I am afraid they will."

Liv broke down to tears and hugged her Dad tightly. She whispered lovingly in his ear, "I promise Daddy." Over the next few months, Liv's Dad's condition would deteriorate quickly. He lost his ability to speak and became very removed and withdrawn. He even began to get agitated when Liv was around and found comfort in his oldest daughter. It was like he was what he had described, an empty vessel, and not the Daddy she remembered. Her Dad only lived a few more months as the battle with cancer was too much for his frail body to withstand.

Several days later, Liv attempted to read the eulogy at her Dad's funeral. In agony, Liv stumbled to tell the story of the late night talks and special times she had with her Dad. Her hands were shaking vigorously and tears were flowing down her cheeks. She felt every breath escaping from her lungs but not returning and felt lightheaded. She uttered the words but it sounded like gibberish as she was crying too deeply. Her sister reached for Liv's hand to console her but it was simply too much. After the funeral, many family members and friends told Liv that they never knew how much her Dad loved history and reading as she had described. They were delighted to learn this about the quiet and reserved man they remembered. Liv knew her secret nights with her Dad would live on forever in her heart and now the hearts of others. She was able to share an amazing part of her inner world with her Dad and she knew he would be proud as well.

Several years passed and Liv found herself honoring her Dad by completing her doctoral program and earning a position as a University Professor. She knew her Dad would be very proud. But despite the time passing, Liv found herself feeling unfulfilled and empty. No matter what she accomplished, the absence of her Dad from her life was too overwhelming. Her Dad was her rock, the earth under her feet, her foundation. She never imagined her life without him. Bouts of anxiety and depression, while not new to Liv, revisited which greatly impacted her relationships, her life, and her feelings about herself. Men seldom stuck around consistently commenting she was too demanding and difficult. Her emotional needs were simply too much for the common man. Liv found herself feeling helpless, hopeless, and fearing she would never feel better again. Headaches were common, insomnia, and panic attacks became so familiar she gave these aspects of her life the name "the three enemies". She often found herself unable to study, feeling disconnected from her body, and unsure of her future.   The loneliness she experienced was taking a toll and she felt like she would never find her way.

Often exhausted, Liv found herself in bed early one night. She began to feel an overwhelming sensation come over her. Was this another panic attack about to happen? She wondered. Her body began to feel heavy and she simply could not move. She tried to yell but was unable to talk. She watched as the room began to move as she felt herself projected into some sort of vortex or tunnel. Then as she began to feel the most fear in her life, she found herself in complete and utter darkness. She was no longer in her bedroom, but she didn't know where she was. Was she dreaming? Losing her mind? Liv's mind was spinning.

Just as she felt she should scream for her life the most amazing calming sensation overcame her. She felt a familiar sensation but couldn't place it. "Hello? Hello? Is anyone here?" she called out to the dark sky demanding someone reply back. "Where am I?" she shouted. Liv began to hear footsteps moving closer to her. "Who is there? I demand you tell me now!" Suddenly, the footsteps stopped. Liv felt an overwhelming sense of loneliness. Liv cried out, "What do you want from me? Why am I here?" Liv fell to the floor sobbing feeling unsure of what was happening to her. Just then, a gentle hand reached on to her shoulder. Surprisingly, Liv did not jump. Instead she touched the top of the hand and recognized it instantly! "Daddy? Is that you?" Liv jumped up from the floor, spun around, and before her eyes was her Dad, Robert standing before her. "How is this possible? Am I dreaming?" she asked.

Her Dad was silent, but their eyes met, and Liv knew this was definitely her Dad. "Why aren't you talking to me, Daddy? What is wrong?" Just in that moment her Dad spoke and said, "You are safe my dear. Please do not fear me." Liv excitedly replied, "Daddy, why am I here? How are you here? Am I dreaming?" Liv's Dad softly answered, "No my love, this is not a dream. I cannot explain it all to you but please know you will be safe." "What do you mean I will be safe?" Liv stuttered? "Am I going somewhere, Daddy?" "Yes, my love, you will be going several places. There is a purpose in these travels my dear. Trust you are taken care of." Nervously, Liv cried out, "Daddy, will I see you again?" "Yes, my love," he replied. "We will see each other again. Just know you are safe and that this is the only way out of the pain for us both."

In that instance, Liv's Dad was gone. Liv fell to the floor, sobbing once again. But this time she was crying out of relief that she had just seen her hero once again. By this time, Liv was exhausted and not knowing what was happening to her, she tried to keep her eyes open but was fading quickly. Liv started to feel that overwhelming sensation come over her again. She was unable to move or to scream. Within a flash, she was back in the tunnel, watching everything spinning. When she woke, she found herself back in her own home, but not in her bedroom. She was in her living room in the chair that she used to sit in with her father when she was a little girl. Liv sobbed for hours yearning to see her Dad again.

CHAPTER 2
TALKING TO THE MOON

∞

Yours is the light by which my spirit is born. You are

my sun, my moon, and all my stars.

-e.e. cummings

Despite seeing her Dad for that brief moment, Liv found herself, years later, stuck in life with no signs of any further journeys. She waited for another sign or to see her Dad again, but nothing happened. Liv found herself becoming further and further removed from everything close to her. The day to day activities became difficult, and she often felt unable to cope. Liv's anxiety levels were at an all-time high leaving her feeling detached from her own self and foggy-brained more days than not. Liv's personal relationships with her friends and family became quite strained and it was as if Liv had become someone completely different. An alter ego of sorts. She began to dress differently and she began to lie about her whereabouts. It was as if she was living a double life no one ever knew about. Liv had moved so far out of her divine feminine energy to spite the pain she felt at the loss of her Dad. Her attachment to her father became replaced with dating men who simply were attracted to her physically with no regard for her inner beauty. She had become someone that even she did not recognize.

Liv continued to attempt to establish a relationship with her mother, Anna, but it was met with great resistance. Every time Liv tried to talk to her Mother about her feelings, fears, or worries, Anna just seemed to push Liv away. It was as if Liv's needs were triggering some unresolved traumas within her Mother. Despite Liv's attempts, Anna grew further and further away from her daughter. Liv felt an immense sense of abandonment and found herself in an abusive relationship. The bright, vibrant, take no shit kind of girl was nowhere to be found. Liv found herself too weak to fight the chronic manipulation, or to even recognize the magnitude of the verbal and physical abuse she was experiencing. Liv faced several visits to the hospital because of the abuse but consistently found her way back in the relationship giving chances and falling victim to empty promises.

It was as if nothing could reach her or awaken her from the space she had slipped into. When Liv was younger, she had been the victim of a date rape. She never told her Dad about the occurrence fearing he would be so angry so she carried the shame and pain from the event to her Mother, Anna. Anna was comforting in this moment assuring Liv that she had been victimized and to not feel shame about this as it was not her fault. For the first time since Liv was very young, she felt an incredible bond and safety in her Mother. Liv's most recent relationship was also a tortured one. After significant physical and verbal abuse, the stress of the abuse was taking a toll on Liv that she found herself awake for twelve days straight. Over the course of these twelve days, she would pass out from exhaustion, but the anxiety would quickly send a jolt through her body to wake her once again.

Despite seeking medical treatment, nothing seemed to help. Liv found herself falling further and further down the rabbit hole of pain and agony. On the twelfth day, Liv found herself crying hysterically in her bed. She knew something had to give but nothing was helping. The lack of sleep was only exacerbating her health and emotional downturn. Needing the support of her Dad, Liv drove to the cemetery back in her hometown. At the cemetery, Liv slumped over her Dad's grave and cried for hours. "Daddy I miss you," cried out Liv. "Please send me a sign that all will be ok. Please, Daddy!" Liv waited but nothing happened. "When are these journeys supposed to happen, Daddy? Why have you not come to me?" Liv felt lost and alone.

Liv left the cemetery and frantically drove home. She could barely make heads or tails of her movements anymore due to her exhaustion. As Liv made it home, she was too tired to go into the house. She found herself sitting on her porch. Feeling the heaviest emotional weight she had ever experienced, she made the decision in her mind that the weight was too much to bear. She had thoughts of leaving this life over the course of the twelve days and tried to fight them. Liv called her Mother to say goodbye. Despite the distance that had emerged in their relationship over the years, Liv's Mother knew something was wrong. She assured Liv this too shall pass and went on to talk about how proud she was of her daughter. She shared many struggles of her own that she had never shared with Liv before. Liv felt an amazing connection with her Mother she hadn't felt in years. After one of the longest conversations she had ever had with her Mother, she sat there in utter silence pondering what she would do next. She knew she didn't want to live like this anymore but her ability to see anything in the future was too dark. Liv became silent. It was as if no more tears could come even if she wanted them to.

It was a late summer night and Liv felt the warm breeze on her face. She looked to the sky and saw it was a full moon. She remembered sitting under the Wise Old Oak in her parents' yard and talking to the Moon. She would tell the Wise Old Oak all about her hopes and dreams. She once asked the Wise Old Oak if anyone was on the other side of the moon listening to her or talking back. She remembered the man her Dad described when she was just a little girl and wondered why he had never shown up. The relationships she had experienced since her Dad's death would certainly not have made her Dad proud, she thought.

As Liv stared into the sky, she said, "Remember me Mr. Moon?" Liv had a beautiful relationship with the sky and air. It was where she found the greatest sense of peace. She began to talk to the Moon. "Did you really hear me when I spoke to you?" She asked the Moon. "I need you more than ever right now. How did I get here?" asked Liv. "What is wrong with me? Why can't I make my head stop spinning?" Liv further went on to say remorsefully, "I know my Dad would be ashamed of me and the choices I have made over these past few years. Please tell him I am sorry." Liv bowed her head and the tears streamed down her cheeks. She knew it was time to go.

As Liv began to get up from her porch, a bright light began to shine over her. It was so bright that she could barely keep her eyes open. Since it was evening, Liv couldn't even imagine where this light was coming from. Her heart was pounding but then slowed immensely. It was as if the sun was shining. Liv sat mesmerized by the light of the sun. She began to feel this amazing warmth come over her. Then suddenly she felt a sense of calm. All the pain in her body had left her consciousness. Then like a flash of light, Liv saw a very large figure appear in front of her. Rubbing her eyes to get a better look through the rays of light, Liv said in a very hoarse voice, "Who are you?"

There was no response. "Who is there? Please respond to me. I know someone is there" cried Liv. "My name is Lucina" replied the woman. "I am the Goddess of Light." Lucina was stunning. She was tall, beautiful, long blonde curly hair well down her back. She had eyes of icy blue water that one could get lost in. "Why are you here" asked Liv. "I am here to take you on a journey," replied Lucina. "The sadness you feel is not you, my dear. The sadness is not for you to bear. There is more for you in this world. You cannot go yet" urged Lucina. "I know your plight well, my dear. My very own Mother grew distant from me and I actually lost the only man I ever loved. I know heartache and pain."

The Goddess was always responsive to the needs of the vulnerable and those who suffered at the hands of the patriarchy. "But there is more for you to see in this life my dear", said Lucina.   Just as she finished her last word, two bright lights began to shine from Lucina's hands. Liv covered her eyes as the lights were incredibly bright. Just as Liv wiped her eyes, she could see two tiny lanterns, one in each hand of Lucina. Lucina presented Liv with the two lanterns. "Do you know what these are, dear one?" asked Lucina. "No, should I?" replied Liv. Lucina walked closer to Liv and said, "These two lanterns represent your future. I have heard you speak to the oak and also to the moon. Why do you fear Motherhood my dear?" Liv bowed her head as her eyes began to well up with tears. "You don't have to hide your eyes from me" softly replied Lucina.

Lucina touched Liv's cheek lovingly and urged her to look at the lanterns. Just as Liv raised her head, she could see energy within the lanterns. It was as if there was life in each one. The blue lantern was glorious with energy that appeared to be dancing. It was just like the energy of thunder as it rolled in the beautiful summer sky after a cleansing rain. Liv felt joy and happiness watching the energy move around. The yellow lantern was beautiful and serene. The energy in this lantern was much more quiet and gentle. Liv felt the most amazing sense of peace looking at the beautiful yellow light. "I fear passing on to my children all that I had to struggle with. My anxiety, my panic, my inability to ever feel comfortable in my own skin. That is no life for a child" cried Liv. Lucina brought the lanterns even closer and sat them down in front of Liv. "What do you feel when you look into the lanterns?" asked Lucina. Liv stuttered with tears in her eyes, "I see beauty and innocence." Lucina softly responded, "These are your children my dear. Do not fear what they will become. Their path is already set and they chose you to be their Mother. They will grow up to do amazing things in this world and you will play a great part in helping them stay to their path. Never doubt this my dear Goddess. Liv touched the lanterns feeling an incredible sense of love and hope in the light.

"We must go" urged Lucina. "Where are we going?" asked Liv. We have a very important journey. In the blink of an eye, the lanterns were gone. "Do not worry my dear, they will be taken care of." Lucina helped Liv up from the ground. In a quiet voice, Liv asked "Do you know my Dad?" Lucina just grinned and said, "Please come with me." Liv once again found herself in the dark tunnel she had seen before. This time she was so exhausted that she began to surrender in the tunnel and decided not to be afraid at her Dad's urging. She felt a beautiful sense of peace wash over her and a loving embrace every time she was in the tunnel. It was as if all of those who came before her and paved the path were watching over her on this journey. Liv began to slowly drift off to sleep.

As Liv awoke, she felt a chill in the air. She called out to Lucina, wondering if she had made the trip with her.

Suddenly, she saw her breath in the air as she called out Lucina's name. "Where am I?" thought Liv. She knew she was somewhere colder than back home but still had no clue as to her specific whereabouts. She began to look around and noticed a small cottage at the top of the hill. There was a little girl walking around and a Mother watching over her. Lucina had made the trip with her, but Liv was still uncertain as to why she was here. Liv continued to look around trying to figure out what she was supposed to be doing in this place. Despite being confused, she marveled in the beauty of the land. It was absolutely breathtaking and everything about it was pristine. There was just enough snow on the branches to look like an image out of a magazine. She had no idea just yet that she was in Iceland...her Mother's native land.

Chapter 3
Out of the Darkness

∞

We are stars wrapped in skin. The light you are seeking has always been within.

-Rumi

To many, Iceland may be a foreign land of mystique and wonder. But not to Liv. Iceland was the homeland of her Mother, Anna. Liv grew up hearing stories about the beautiful land and culture of Iceland and its people. Liv fell in love with the pictures of the Northern Lights or Aurora Borealis and always dreamed of visiting the place her Mother called Home as a little girl. Even though Liv and her Mother were close when she was very young, Anna found Liv emotionally challenging. As Liv grew older, Anna became more agitated and told her daughter that she simply felt frustrated and began to withdraw further. Fortunately, Liv had her Dad to connect with, but as any little girl who feels a void between herself and her Mother, Liv constantly sought validation and acceptance from Anna.

At this point in her life, and after many failed attempts at relationships, Liv began to wonder if love would ever find her. She was also now in her 30s and began to think about the possibility of children of her own. However, Liv always feared Motherhood. Not only did she struggle to understand her own Mother, but she worried she would somehow create pain in her children's lives by passing on her anxiety, depression, and awkwardness. Despite these concerns, she did dream of a family one day. She used to cut out pictures of families and children and make cards to give to people. Liv and her Dad would tell the Wise Old Oak all about the family she yearned for with one boy and one girl running around in the yard for the Wise Old Oak to talk to. As Liv grew older, she became restless and the dream seemed to move further and further back into the recesses of her mind.

After waking up in Iceland, Liv asked Lucina why they were there. Lucina told Liv all about a little girl who lived in a town just up the way they were to visit. The weather wasn't too cold and Liv was in awe of the beauty of Iceland. "This is just as my Mother described," said Liv. It was late but it was still light outside. It seemed as though it was the time of year when one could experience light well into the midnight hour. Liv welcomed the light after experiencing the immense dark hole she had been in for the last few years. Liv and Lucina began to walk toward the small village near the water.

Liv was surprised at how peaceful the land was. Her Mother, Anna had told her many stories about growing up in Iceland, but it always seemed as though there was something missing from her stories. An emptiness of sorts. Anna never spoke about friends or the things that she loved the most about growing up here. She just simply spoke of the land or typical experiences. As Liv and Lucina arrived at the small town, Liv noticed a little girl playing by the water. Considering how late it was, Liv wondered why such a little girl would be out all alone. The little girl's Mother called for her and she ran to the house. "Who is that little girl, Lucina?" asked Liv. Lucina whispered, "Look closely, dear one." Just as Liv and the little girl's eyes met, she knew it was her mother, Anna. "How are we even here" uttered Liv. "How could this be?" Lucina remained quiet as to force Liv to pay attention to the little girl.

Over the next several days, Liv was able to observe her Mother as a little girl. She saw the comings and goings of Anna and how she led a pretty isolated life. Anna's Mother was quite protective of her and didn't take her eyes off of her except to do her chores. It was like the most beautiful cage one could ever be placed in here in Iceland. Little Anna just seemed to do as she was told. She wasn't a vibrant, energetic child. She seemed quite calm for a little one. Liv quickly flashed back to when she was Little Anna's age. She remembers playing by herself for hours in her bedroom and seeing her guides and angels within the reflection of the mirror. It was as if they were there to protect her and to assure her that she would always be taken care of. Liv never felt alone as she always knew of the presence and love of these guides. Liv wondered who was taking care of Little Anna.

One day, Liv was watching Little Anna and heard Anna's Mother yell out that they needed to go into town. Little Anna became quite unsettled and began throw a temper tantrum. Liv was surprised at what she was seeing. After all, Anna had barely spoken in the short time that Liv was able to see her. Little Anna became so restless that she ran down to the water. Weeping uncontrollably, Liv reached her hand on to the shoulder of Little Anna startling her. "I am sorry" said Liv. "Please don't be afraid. My name is Olivia, but you can call me Liv." Anna's eyes lit up as though she recognized Liv. "Why are you crying?" asked Liv. Little Anna sat quietly unsure of how to respond. She replied, "I can't go. I can't go." Liv touched her hand softly and asked her where she couldn't go. Little Anna went on to tell Liv about a man in town who owned a shoe store who was hurting her. Liv became quite upset, but masked it so that she wouldn't scare Little Anna. "Please tell me what you mean by hurting you. How does this man hurt you?" asked Liv. Little Anna became very nervous and couldn't make eye contact. She seemed to definitely be uncomfortable and wanting to stop talking. In that moment, Little Anna's Mother called for her and off she ran.

Just then, Lucina appeared before Liv. She appeared to be floating over the water. Just like the angel Liv's Dad used to tell her all about when she was little. "I know the pain you are feeling dear one. It is hard to see the hurt of others and feel as though you are helpless. You are not helpless. There is a divine purpose for this journey. Look within and you will know what to do." Liv and Lucina continued on through the small town and came under the northern lights. "It is stunning" said Liv. "My Mother told me that she used to sit by the water and look at the sky for hours. I always wondered why she never spoke of her friends or the things she loved and I think I am beginning to see why. This is no way for a young child to live. She should be playing and not full of fear."

Lucina told Liv that she had a very special gift for her. She held out her hand and presented Liv with a beautiful shiny object. It was a sword. "What is that?" asked Liv. Lucina replied, "this is a very special sword my dear. It is the sword of Freya. A Norse Goddess of love but also known as the deity of war and death. Legend has it that Freya's twin brother, Freyr, went into battle but forgot his sword and perished as he exchanged his sword for the hand of his love. Freya, however, despite being depicted with the sword in many images, decided to stay out of the war recognizing that while she may be the Goddess of war and death, she was also the deity of love and beauty. She chose a more peaceful path than war but she is often seen in images with this sword. It was as if the sword was her protector, yet she found her own way out of the duality. Take this sword as my gift. It will help you find your way. It is also known to have great powers to fight on its own." Liv was in awe of the special gift given to her by Lucina. She stared at the sword for hours wishing she would be able to live up to the legacy of those who had carried this before her.

The next day, Liv was back in the small town looking for little Anna but she was nowhere to be found. Liv saw Little Anna's mother hanging close by the water and wondered what could have happened to Little Anna? Later that evening, Little Anna finally emerged from inside her small cottage on the water. She was sitting under the stars and looking into the sky. Liv approached Little Anna gingerly and sat down next to her. "My Dad used to tell me about an angel in the sky who would always watch over me. I asked my angel if she would watch over you now" whispered Liv. Little Anna began to cry. "What is wrong?" asked Liv. Liv could see some dark marks on Anna's arms and legs peeking out from under her dress. Little Anna quickly covered the marks. "Did that man do this to you?" asked Liv. Little Anna just wept. Liv tenderly put her hand on her shoulder and asked Little Anna if she could give her a hug. Little Anna nodded and the two embraced. "No one should ever hurt you like this" cried Liv. You are a beautiful little girl who should be playing and enjoying her childhood." The two spent more than an hour together as Little Anna found great comfort with Liv. It was as if she looked to her as her very own Mother in a way. However, it was getting late and Little Anna's Mother called for her and off she ran back up the hill to her cottage.

Despite having one of the most joyous moments of her life with Little Anna, Liv became so enraged she could barely breathe. She began to tremble inside and felt like her head was spinning. She felt a deep inner calling to protect Little Anna as if she were her own child. Was she here to protect Little Anna from this man? All Liv could think about was making sure that Little Anna was never hurt again. She knew her purpose in Iceland had to be related to this man but she wasn't quite sure of exactly what to do.

Liv quickly got up from the ground and called out in the loudest voice she had ever used in her life, "LUCINA!

LUCINA! I NEED YOU NOW! PLEASE LUCINA, WHERE ARE YOU? In a flash, Lucina appeared before Liv. "What is wrong my dear?" asked Lucina. "I must find that man" cried Liv. "The one who hurt Little Anna?" questioned Lucina. "Yes. So you know?" said Liv. Lucina moved closely to Liv and whispered in her ear, "Yes, my dear. I am sorry you had to see that but this is why you are here. I cannot tell you what to do. You must go within and find the answers you seek." Instead, Liv ran up the hill and into town. She began to search for the man everywhere. She remembered Little Anna mentioning something about a shoe repair store. Liv searched and found the store but it was closed. The lights were off and there was no one in the front of the store. Just as Liv began to walk away, a light suddenly switched on and there stood the man that hurt Little Anna. Liv began to breathe heavily. Her heart was pounding and she felt sick to her stomach.

Liv knew she had to do something. She couldn't bear seeing Little Anna hurt or full of fear. Liv remembered what Lucina had mentioned about looking within, but Liv's temper often got the best of her when she felt helpless or hurt.

Instead of looking within, Liv ran to the back of the store to see if there was another way to get into the store. She was surprised to see a stairwell headed down into the basement. A lantern hung at the top of the stairwell and was simply too bright to ignore. Liv ran down the stairs and into the unlocked basement of the building. As Liv entered the basement she was surprised to see a small apartment. It appeared that someone lived in this cold, damp space. "Who would live here?" Liv asked herself. It seemed unfit to be a home for anyone. It was dark and no place for anyone to live she thought in her mind.

Liv continued to snoop around the room to see what she could find. She found very little. In fact, there were only a few articles of clothes, very little food, and a few candles to provide lighting. As Liv looked a bit further, she became mesmerized by a book that was on what appeared to be a dusty table. It looked like someone was writing a manuscript or beginning a diary of some sort. She scoured each page of the book reading all about the stories of a young boy who faced pain and scrutiny at the hands of the Father he loved.

The author went on to describe horrible experiences of abuse and torture. Just then Liv realized the apartment belonged to the man who was hurting Little Anna. "How could he write this book?" she thought. "He is a monster playing the victim through his words, yet still hurting Little Anna."

Liv became further enraged and suddenly felt something near her waist. Liv ran her thin fingers over the belt of her skirt, feeling a cold, sharp object. It was the sword Lucina gave her. She couldn't believe she had forgotten about the sword. In that instance, Liv couldn't stop her head from spinning and her insides from trembling. Just in that moment, Liv pulled out the sword and ran back up the stairs. She went to the front of the store, hiding the sword behind her back. Liv knocked at the door, and the man yelled "We are closed. Come back tomorrow." Liv cried out, "I am sorry, Sir. Please let me in, I fell down the stairs and think I hurt myself." The man shouted yet again, "Ma'am I am sorry, but we are closed. I cannot help you." The man moved to the door and saw Liv standing outside. Their eyes met and the man changed his mind and opened the door. In one swift swoop, Liv pushed herself into the store knocking the man on the ground. Liv charged the door with the energy of a fierce lioness.

The man was stunned and lay on the floor. Liv placed her foot on top of the chest of the man and pointed the sword at his neck. "Do you know why am I here?" snarled Liv. The man didn't speak a word, he was too frightened to speak and just looked into Liv's eyes. "There is a little girl that you have hurt. She is a very special little girl to me. No one hurts those I love" shouted Liv. She continued her outburst, "I know one thing for sure...you will never hurt her again!" The man was shaking vigorously and tried to utter a few words. "Quiet!" said Liv. "I will decide when you get to talk and in my eyes, YOU have said enough through your actions." Liv began to have flash backs to being bullied when she was a little girl. The anger intensified as she started to push the sword down even closer to the man's skin. Liv stumbled to speak, "I was bullied as a little girl and no one protected me. I will be damned if she (referring to Little Anna) will ever have to look at you again or feel fear of any kind." In that instance the man cried out, "please...please stop! I am sorry. I never meant to hurt her." It was obvious that the man knew who Liv was referring to.

"Something happens in my head and I can't seem to stop the rage." The man began to cry profusely, shaking like a frightened little boy. He then stuttered in fear, "I will never hurt anyone again. I am sorry. Please God forgive me for all that I have done."

Liv began to think of all the pain she felt as a child being bullied by others and how helpless she felt. In that moment, Liv took her foot off of the man, lifted the tip of the sword away from his neck, and let out a huge exhale. It was as if she breathed out her entire childhood trauma into that room. She slowly backed away from the man but never took her eyes off of him. The man didn't move as he was certain if he did, Liv knew how to use that sword. He had never faced the wrath of a woman in that way and wasn't going to take a chance with his life.

Liv was not only a warrior, but a Professor of Psychology. She knew the lasting imprint childhood abuse had on its victims. The patterns of brutality either show through fear or anger. The man who hurt Little Anna was textbook. She felt a deep desire to try to help the man, but she wasn't here to diagnose him, she knew that for sure. She was here to try to protect Little Anna to rewrite her childhood story. Liv also hoped in doing so, that she could save her own relationship with her Mother as well. Liv left the store calling on Lucina. "Lucina, please help me" she whispered. Lucina was nowhere to be found. As Liv made her way back to the top of the hill, she saw Little Anna and Lucina sitting by the water star gazing. Little Anna was laughing and seemed happier than ever. Liv walked up slowly and placed her hand on Little Anna's shoulder. "It is lovely to see you smile, beautiful girl." said Liv joyously. Little Anna reached out to Liv and hugged her tightly. Lucina told me that it is time for you to leave. Thank you for protecting me. You are my hero. Every time I see that angel in the sky, I will remember her as Liv" said Little Anna. Just as quickly as they embraced, Little Anna ran up the hill and waved goodbye.

"Oh, Lucina. I am speechless. Did I do what I was supposed to?" asked Liv. Lucina softly commented, "There is no one right way to anything my dear. There is only 'a' way. You found the sword and used it to help you find your courage, but you quickly found that it wasn't courage, that you needed to change this situation...it was Compassion. Even the mightiest of men can face brutality and pain. Boys who are hurt grow into men who hurt. It is a vicious cycle." Liv began to reflect on the attitudes and perceptions of men she had encountered over the years. She remembered the hurt, betrayal, and abandonment she had felt and suddenly was able to feel the hurt, betrayal, and agony of the men. It was so overwhelming that she fell to her knees. "Make it stop, Lucina! Make it stop!" Lucina brought out the lanterns. Liv became quiet and asked if she could hold the lanterns. "Of course", said Lucina. "They would love to see their Mother."

Liv took the lanterns and walked over to the water. She gracefully set them down and watched their vibrant energy playing within the lanterns. Liv lovingly began to talk to her children. "I cannot wait to be with you permanently my dear children. I promise you I will never let anyone or anything harm you or get in your way of living the best life you are destined for. You, my beloveds, will want for nothing, you will never search in vain, and you will never feel needless pain. I swear my life on this oath I make to you." The lights of the lanterns began to shine brighter than they ever did before. Liv felt an immense sense of relief and calm knowing the fear she had of being a Mother could be put to rest. Not only had she become the protector and surrogate Mother of Little Anna, but she had surrendered the anger she had felt toward men to this point and felt love and compassion for the man who was hurting Little Anna.

Liv began to walk back to Lucina with her children. "What will happen to them now?" asked Liv. Lucina smiled and said, "I swear to you they will be taken care of with all of my honor. They have waited a lifetime for you" said Lucina. "When will I see them again?" whispered Liv. "When you are ready my dear" replied Lucina. There is more for you to see and do." "Am I going on another journey, Lucina?" "Yes, my dear" said Lucina. "It is time for you to go. However, you are going to face even a greater challenge in your next journey. I know in my soul that you are the most beautiful Goddess I have ever laid eyes on. Your heart is golden and your soul is pure. Nothing can hurt you, my darling. All is taken care of." Just in that instance, Lucina kissed Liv on her forehead and hugged her gently. "I am always with you. Look within and you will find me" whispered Lucina and off she went into the Northern Lights.

Liv had tears in her eyes as she reflected upon her time in Iceland. This time the tears were of happiness and relief. With each passing journey, Liv was releasing and surrendering aspects that once caused her immense pain. She was finding her true self and beginning to believe in her path once again. If only her Dad could see her now. He would be so proud, she thought. Liv looked up to the sky and saw her Dad's favorite constellation, Orion. She began to speak to her Dad. "Daddy, I have no idea what impact my time here in Iceland will have on my relationship with Mother, but know I have found that feeling inside of me once again. That feeling of life and purpose. I will never let that light go out again. I promise you Daddy."

As she stared into the sky, everything started to move. Liv knew it was time to leave. She simply took a deep breath knowing she was safe. She closed her eyes and sent loving energy into Iceland and said goodbye. In a flash, Liv was in the tunnel of darkness on her way to her next journey. She began to wonder where she was headed.

Wherever she was headed, she knew this was the most challenging battle per Lucina's urging. Instead of worrying, Liv looked within and meditated to find the answers. Liv began to feel an incredible pain in her leg. She saw a hospital in her mind. It appeared to be a surgical room. Was something going to happen to her Mother? Liv was quickly startled awake and noticed she was back in her home. As Liv moved toward her window to see what was going on, she noticed it was definitely cold outside by the frost that was evident on her window. When she left for Iceland it was still Fall. The leaves were beautiful and the temperature still mild. It was definitely colder and no leaves were left on the trees.

Liv began to see lights flashing across the street. She noticed the sign said "Seasons Greetings." It was Christmas time! She thought. Immediately her phone rang and it was her Mother, Anna. "Are you ready?" asked Anna. "Ready for what, Mother?" "Ready to go shopping! Your Godmother and God Sister are in town. Did you forget?" said Anna. "No way. I am excited." said Liv excitedly. "I can't wait to see you all."

Chapter 4

Nothing is Everything

∞

As above
So below
As the Universe
So the Soul
As without
So within
-Hermes

Christmas was Liv's favorite time of the year. The sparkle and beauty of the festive lights often illuminated the sky of the dark winters. Liv was able to feel the energy of the people as they prepared for the holiday season. It just seemed as though people were happier and more joyful this time of year. Liv's family was in town for the holidays and things seem to be pretty positive overall. Liv and her Mother were getting along well and making plans for the festivities to take place over the next few weeks. Anna even offered to take Liv to her annual dermatology appointment coming up. Anna knew that Liv often became nervous about the skin checks since her Dad had died from cancer. However, Anna was very supportive and went along willingly.

Liv's porcelain skin was quite delicate and she never seemed to age. Despite being in her mid-thirties now, many often commented on how she seemed to be moving backward in time and looking younger every time one saw her. Liv was learning to accept compliments, but still felt a bit uneasy when people were overly affectionate or indulgent about her physical beauty.

It seemed as though Liv had become quite sensitive to the possibility of death after losing her father several years prior. Her father was only 58 when he passed and this certainly stayed at the front of Liv's mind as she was getting older. Liv remembered when her Dad would often talk about how his Mother and Sister died very young. He always feared he would die young as well. And he did. But Liv was diligent about her doctors' appointments and stayed on top of her health. Liv arrived at her dermatologist's office as she always had in December. Her doctor was quite kind and they always had several moments of fun conversation about their lives before the exam began. He would often speak of his children which often made Liv sad or uneasy in the past. However, she welcomed the conversation and even asked her doctor how old his children were now. Her doctor certainly took notice of Liv's interest and asked how she was feeling these days. Liv commented that she felt good overall and was looking forward to the holidays with her family.

Liv's Doctor proceeded to ask if she had noticed any changes to her skin. Just in that instance Liv was about to comment that she had not seen anything different, but as she looked down at her legs, a bright light began to shine from her right shin area. "Did you see that, Doc?" Cried out Liv. "No," said her doctor. "What did you see?" Liv went on to describe how she must be going crazy but she saw a light on the front of her right leg. Her doctor proceeded to do a full body scan but didn't seem overly worried about anything. Liv commented, "what about the freckle on my right shin?" Her doctor took a look but didn't seem impressed, but suddenly he stopped. He became quiet. He said it seemed as though it had appeared out of nowhere. He said he didn't remember seeing the freckle before and that it did seem a bit odd. Liv's Doctor took a sample of the tissue and told her they would follow up in a week or two. But no news was good news. Liv left the appointment and told her Mother what had happened. Anna reminded her to not let the worry consume her day and to release the worry until she heard further from the doctor. Liv agreed and on they went to enjoy their day together.

Holiday planning continued on for Liv and her family. In fact, Liv was so busy that she didn't even notice that she hadn't heard from the doctor's office about her skin biopsy. In fact, ten days had passed. It was a week before Christmas and Liv was shopping with her family at the local mall. The weather was perfect, the music was playing, and all was feeling amazing in the world. Just then, Liv's phone ran and it was the doctor's office. Liv froze and simply couldn't get her hand to accept the call. Instead, she sent it to voicemail. It was as if she already knew the outcome of the call. After several failed attempts, the phone rang again. Reluctantly, Liv finally answered.

The nurse indicated the doctor had attempted to reach her but had left for the holiday. The nurse asked Liv if she was alone. "No. I am with my family" replied Liv. "Oh good" said the nurse. "Can you sit down to talk for a few minutes?" requested the nurse. Liv sat down reluctantly, clutching her purse in her other hand. As the fateful words were spoken, Liv lost awareness of her present surroundings. It was as if someone was talking to her in a tunnel. "The nurse indicated the office would be in touch after Christmas to arrange the surgery and additional treatments. Liv's hands began to shake. She was not sure what had happened to her, but she knew the reality of death she had always feared was present and alive in front of her. "Why now?" she thought. Everything had been so positive since her return from Iceland. She and Anna were closer than ever and she was looking forward to her future. She began to panic remembering her children. "Will I still get to see my children?" she screamed out loud. "Lucina! What is happening to me?" She decided to go meditate as Lucina had recommended. She needed her now more than ever.

After several minutes of deep breathing and quiet, Liv began to focus on the rhythm of her heartbeat. She then saw the beautiful Lucina within her. "Oh Lucina, what is happening to me? Is this the challenge you referred to?" "All is taken care of my dear" replied Lucina. "What will happen to my children?" cried Liv. "I gave you my word, dear one. Your beloveds are safe and sound. They will see you soon. Now stay present and do what is asked of you. You will find the next journey very soon." Liv opened her eyes and took a deep breath of relief knowing her children were ok. Over the next several months, Liv would face several surgeries to extract the cancerous tissue, skin grafts to fill and repair the leg, and countless hours in therapy facing her mortality. Liv began to worry each day that the cancer could come back, show up in a different part of her body, or simply make her unable to function through the day's most basic events. She watched her Dad die of cancer, and it had become her greatest fear. Over the next year, Liv would be informed that she also had a mysterious mass in her left kidney. She began to see yet another doctor regarding this new concern. After several tests and office visits, it was determined that the doctor would simply observe the mass for the time being to see if it would change shape or size. Liv tried to be optimistic about this somewhat unadventurous news, but something inside was ringing with pessimism.

Anna seemed to have a very special place in her heart for Liv now. She saw her daughter struggling with the cancer diagnoses and asked her if they could talk. Of course Liv jumped at the chance to have time with her Mother. They spoke for hours about Anna's own insecurities, fears, and worries over the last several decades. Anna went on to share with Liv how she felt that she gave up 40 years of her life worrying about many things that either never happened or were insignificant to her purpose in life. Anna placed her hand on Liv's and told her that she had one wish for her daughter. "Please don't waste your life worrying about things that aren't for certain. And even if they were certain, there is always free will to change one's impact on the outcome. You are braver than you know and I know no matter what you have to face, that you will face it with grace. You are beautiful my daughter. You will not die. I see you well and old holding your grandchildren. Embrace this and live. Please live." Liv smiled admirably at her Mother. She knew the mountains of abuse and anxiety she had to face as a little girl. Liv knew she never wished any of this for her own children and needed to truly do something to move out of this space of insecurity and doubt.

Despite reminding herself of the words of Lucina that all was taken care of, no matter what she did she simply couldn't shake the fear of dying. Was it her connection to her father or was it something else rooting her in this relentless and crippling fear? Liv couldn't make heads or tails of her emotions. She just knew it was simply becoming too much to bear. Liv felt like the darkness was returning. She promised her Dad that she would never let the light dim again. Yet, she felt she was fading back into the shadow within. That day she

eached out to her therapist who made room on the schedule
o see her the very next day. Liv was exhausted and headed to
bed.

That night, Liv tossed and turned for hours. She looked
out her window and spoke to the Wise Old Oak. "Oh Wise
One, why is this happening to me again? Just as I get out of
the darkness, it returns to remind me it isn't done with me."
The Wise Old Oak reminded Liv that she was a Goddess. "Look
within dear. Your strength lies in your ability to see what I
have seen all of this time. I have watched you grow and
overcome all that was before you dear one." Liv said
goodnight to Wise Old Oak and began to say her prayers. As
she prayed to Mother Mary, she quickly felt her eyes get
heavy and felt the all too common tunnel feeling and room
spinning. She knew she was off to the journey Lucina had
mentioned. She prayed that she would be strong enough to
find her way through this one. Liv was beyond exhausted, and
in an instance she was off to sleep.

Liv woke up and was in the darkness once again. It
seemed to be a common theme. These journeys ended in

complete and utter darkness. But why? Liv's father had told her to not worry about these journeys, but she still hadn't been able to piece together the puzzle of exactly why these journeys were occurring. That was until this journey. Liv began to walk around and noticed she was not in a typical structure like a house or building. In fact, Liv noticed that she was inside of a cave. Why was she here? In a cave of all places? She continued walking following the light and air that she could feel on her skin. She found her way to the entrance of the cave.

Outside the cave there was snow and what appeared to be a very tall mountainous range. She remembered her journey to Iceland with Lucina, but this was definitely not Iceland with the vast mountainous range. Just then Liv began to cry out, "Hello? Is anyone here? Please, I have been on these journeys long enough to know there is a guide. Please show yourself to me. Please," she cried. Just then a huge shadow began to move closer to her. Liv was very cold but all of a sudden felt warm again. "Who are you?" she uttered.

A very tall, muscular, figure stood before her. His eyes were closed. He didn't speak a word. Yet, within a moment, Liv began to hear him speak. How are you doing that? Why am I able to hear you? Yet your lips aren't moving? "Shush", he said. Liv became silent. And in a very loud and commanding voice, he said, "I am The Destroyer. You are about to face your most challenging journey yet. Are you ready my child?" Liv wasn't sure how she felt about the challenge but always remembered the words of her Dad, "you will be going several places. There is a purpose in these travels my dear. Trust you are taken care of." Just then, Liv caught a glimpse of a shiny object behind The Destroyer. After the battle Liv faced in Iceland, she still felt somewhat depleted from her valiant effort to fight the patriarchy. Liv began to look around the cave as the Destroyer continued to speak to her. Her eyes moved back and forth, up and down, hoping for any sign of understanding of what she was about to face.

Liv's eyes came upon a majestic item in the right hand of the Destroyer. She asked him what he was holding. The Destroyer responded, "This is त्रिशूल *triśūl*, it represents all of creation and destruction, law and order, mind, body, and spirit. The world here, the world below, and the world beyond." Liv remembered hearing stories of Gods who fought battles with tridents from her Dad. She slowly moved toward the object and recognized it instantly. "What is that you are carrying my dear?" asked The Destroyer. Liv became confused and replied, "I am not carrying anything." The Destroyer smiled and said, "Are you sure, my child?" Liv looked down and noticed a shiny object hanging to the left of her waist. It was her sword. Liv had forgotten all about her sword that she used for her battle in Iceland. "I didn't realize I was carrying this with me." replied Liv. The Destroyer quickly responded, did you ever truly put it down?" "What?" Asked Liv. "What do you mean?" The Destroyer quickly reminded Liv that she had been carrying the fears of death and dying and everything that she was conditioned to believe about mortality within her soul. That she hadn't truly surrendered. "How can I surrender if I am facing the possibility of dying?" cried out Liv. "You are the Mother of all, my dear", replied The Destroyer. "Why do you deny yourself the right to see your own divine power? Put down your sword my child."

Liv looked down at her leg and reminded The Destroyer of her cancer. "I am not making this up", she said. "I have gone through surgeries and pain because of this battle." In that moment, Liv looked up and realized The Destroyer was gone. "Where did you go?" screamed out Liv. "Why did you leave me?" Suddenly Liv felt a blustery cold breeze blow over her. She knew she wasn't alone. She continued to the cry out to The Destroyer but heard no reply. Instead she saw an enormous three-headed dragon flying toward her. Liv swiftly lifted her sword from her waist, and ran as fast as she could to find shelter. Liv's heart was pounding and she was praying that she would fall asleep and awaken somewhere else. However, she remained here realizing there was something more to this experience. Just as the three-headed dragon reappeared, she noticed the images of all those who had betrayed her, hurt her, or abandoned her over the years appear on the faces of the dragon. Liv was flooded with terror and uncertainty. She fell to the ground having to face all that she thought she had left behind. Why was she having to face these enemies at this point of the journey? Just then The Destroyer appears and quickly called to her, "Liv, my child, you need to get up." "I can't", she cried out. "I need your help...PLEASE!!!!" The Destroyer said he could not fight this battle for her, and that she had to look within for what she was seeking.

Liv closed her eyes hoping she would just fall to sleep but it wasn't time. Liv became agitated and watched her hands tremble in terror. She suddenly heard a whisper in her ear, a man's voice, "you are all that you seek my dear. This is not you. The fear, the worry, the belief you can't fight is simply not you. Stand up!" Liv stood to her feet, sword in hand and began to move toward the three-headed dragon. With anger in her bones, she quickly lashed out at the one head of the dragon. She fell to the ground once again. But to Liv's amazement, the head regenerated. Liv couldn't believe what she was seeing. She stood to her feet and swung at another head and it happened again. They just kept regenerating no matter how hard she fought. The man's voice repeated, "You are all that you seek my dear, only you can see this. Now look within!" Liv looked around but realized there was no one with her once again. Then she felt a tender touch on her shoulder and she took a deep breath to settle herself.

With the sword in her hand she approached the three-headed dragon once again and with a gentle exhale, she closed her eyes, and saw the most beautiful light that was within, and said to herself "As far I stood, within my vessel. I rise above, like a dove of white. As darkness on the horizon, bows down to the dawn. And with these words, comes the beauty of this sight. I put down my sword, as there's nothing there to fight. Let dust meet dust and let light be thy light." The cave was suddenly illuminated by light more beautiful and powerful than the northern lights and the three-headed dragon was obliterated to nothing more than dust. Liv fell to the ground, exhausted. She cried out to the man who was speaking to her but he never appeared. Instead, The Destroyer reappeared and Liv asked where he had been. The Destroyer reminder Liv that he was within her. "I am always with you, replied The Destroyer. "You did this all alone with your strength and your light. Do you still not see your own divine power?"

The Destroyer demanded Liv to walk over to the icy wall of the cave. Still emotional from the battle, Liv reluctantly walked over the icy wall of the cave and asked what she was supposed to see. Be patient, Liv. You will see. Just then Liv was able to see her reflection in the mirror. However, she was able to see all of the scars from her skin cancer. "Why do you want me to look at the scars?" cried out Liv. The Destroyer commented, "These scars are not you. These scars are not separate aspects of your physical body. The scars represent the path and all that you went through to get to this moment. They are nothing to be ashamed of or hide from. If you continue to hide, I cannot guarantee you will not have to face this battle again." Liv cried out, "I am so tired. I have had enough!" "Have you?" Asked The Destroyer? "Look at your reflection again. Tell me what is God to you?" Liv was frustrated and spoke about her beliefs about God and her love for God. The Destroyer patiently said, "I will ask you one more time, what is God to you?" As she looked within the mirror, all of her guides appeared within her reflection. Liv began to cry. 'I' AM GOD, she shouted. GOD IS ME." "Yes my child" replied the Destroyer. As Liv looked into the mirror she noticed her scars were gone. "Where did they go", asked Liv? The Destroyer said "nowhere, Liv." Liv cried out, "The scars are still there. Why can't I see them?" "Because you have surrendered to the need to see them, lovingly replied The Destroyer. When you honor the Divine essence of your soul, you will only see that which is truly you."

Liv spent some time looking at the reflection, feeling a great sense of calm, she felt as though she had truly surrendered to all that she had feared before the beginning of this journey. Just in that moment The Destroyer walked to the edge of the cave. Liv chased after him to see where he was going. The Destroyer pointed to her waist and said, "Will you be needing that any longer my child?" Liv looked down and was surprised to see, she still had the sword attached to her waist. "I thought I let this down in the battle?" she said with confusion. "There was no battle my child." In that moment, Liv handed the sword to The Destroyer quietly exhaling "I am all I need, Father." The Destroyer smiled with loving joy. Just then The Destroyer walked back into the cave. "Will I ever see you again", shouted Liv? The Destroyer replied, "I am within you my dear. Look inside if you ever need me." He took his meditative position and Liv walked out of the cave. Noticing how exhausted she was, she also sat down and decided to meditate and rest before her return home. Within minutes, Liv's eyes became heavy and she felt her surroundings beginning to move. She knew it was time to leave. This time, she forced her eyes open to get one last glimpse of The Destroyer. He was peaceful and content. Liv smiled and fell asleep.

CHAPTER 5
JUST BE

∞

At a distance you only see my light.

Come closer and know that I am you.

-Rumi

L iv woke up from her deep sleep. She knew she had left the cold Himalayas as she immediately felt the warm breeze gently blow through her long, blonde hair. Liv had become quite accustomed to these journeys despite the after effects to her body. But this time felt different. Liv jumped to her feet and began to look around to try to find out her location. She was shocked to find that she was laying outside under the stars. She looked up into the sky and saw the constellation of Orion. She remembered this from her meeting with Lucina. But she knew she wasn't in Iceland as the weather was too warm, especially at night time. Liv ran to the street to see what she could find. There were a few people walking around in a park, but they didn't seem to be speaking English. She recognized by the beautiful clothing of the women that she was in India.

Liv had a deep love for the country of India and had several friends from the country. However, she was petrified to be in yet another place with possibly no way to communicate with others. Liv's hands began to shake. But just in that moment, she remembered the words of her Dad, that she was safe and to not fear these journeys. Liv took some deep breaths, closed her eyes, and began to pray. Mother Mary, if you can hear me, I am not sure of my purpose in this moment, but I trust all will be presented to me in time. Please keep me safe and help me to find my divine purpose on this journey. As Liv slowly opened her eyes, she found a man standing before her. "Miss, are you ok?" He said quietly. "You speak English?" Exclaimed Liv. "Ummm...yes, I hope that was English" as the man calmly let out a gentle laugh. "My name is Raj. What is your name Miss?" "My...my name is Liv", she stuttered. "Can you help me?" said Liv quietly. "Yes, Miss Liv. I saw you sitting in the park and something or someone told me to stop. It was like a woman's voice insisting I stop and there you were." Liv knew Mary had heard her prayer. "Raj, where am I?" asked Liv. "You are in Jaipur, India Miss Liv. I take it you have never been to India before? "No...never" Liv said as she began to feel nervous. "It's ok Miss Liv. I will help you. Have you eaten?" "No. I haven't" said Liv. "Well let's get to that."

Raj was very kind to Liv and helped her into the small car. They proceeded to drive around in search of food, and Raj stayed with Liv watching over her like a hawk. Liv began to wonder if Raj was her guide for this journey. "Do you have any idea why you are here Miss Liv?" Asked Raj. "Honestly, I don't." Just as Liv went to open up her phone to check the time, Raj saw the picture on her screen. "Miss Liv, you have been here before", shouted Raj. "I certainly have not", argued Liv. "The tree Miss Liv...the tree. That tree is here in Jaipur." Liv was stunned and lost for words. She looked down at her phone and saw the picture of Wise Old Oak that she grew up with at her childhood house. "This is a tree in my parents' yard", said Liv. "Wow!" Said Raj. "It looks identical to a tree here in Jaipur. In fact, said Raj, "the tree is quite the attraction. It sits alone in this slab of concrete. Many refer to it as the Wise Old Sage, or Saadhoo." "Why is that?" Asked Liv. Raj went on to tell the many stories of people who sought the guidance of the Old Sage for many of life's struggles. "Raj, can you take me there?" "Of course Miss Liv. I thought you would never ask." Raj and Liv raced off to see the Old Oak tree.

As Raj and Liv were driving, Liv noticed a heavy smell in the air and that it seemed rather smoky. "Raj, why is it so smoky?" "We just celebrated Diwali, Miss Liv. Crackers are quite common during the celebration." "Why crackers?" Asked Liv. Raj went on to tell her all about the festival of lights and the spiritual victory of light over darkness, good over evil and knowledge over ignorance. Liv was mesmerized by the love Raj had when talking about India. She knew she had a different purpose with this trip but just couldn't figure it out just yet. Just then, Raj pulled up to the concrete slab. Raj wasn't kidding. The Old Oak was standing all alone and it looked exactly like the tree in Liv's parents' yard. "I told you Miss Liv", said Raj. "You definitely weren't kidding Raj. Thank you for taking me here." "I will wait for you in the park Miss Liv." "No, Raj. I have to do this alone." "What do you need to do Miss Liv?" Asked Raj. "It's a long story, Raj. But please accept my sincerest gratitude for the kindness and generosity you have shown me. You are a beautiful soul dear Raj, Namaste." "Namaste, Miss Liv. Please take care of yourself. I wish you well."

As Raj sped away, Liv found herself alone in India. She had a suspicion that Raj was not her guide for this journey and began to look around the area of the tree. Liv noticed the top of the tree was damaged. It looked as though it had been impacted by the smoke. "I hope the tree will be ok", Liv thought. Something felt right about the location, but Liv still didn't know why she was even in India. Liv was getting tired and decided to lay under the Old Sage. It was now morning. She faithfully awaited the next guide, but more time had passed. Day turned into night and there she was yet again, under the stars. She had flash backs to the many conversations she had with the Moon as a little girl. Liv became restless and decided to close her eyes. Just as she began to relax she heard the voice of the Old Sage speaking to her. But it was the voice she remembered of the tree in her parent's house. How could the tree have the same voice? "Hello?" She cried out. "Is anyone there? Please….are you there?"

Liv sat in silence praying the tree would talk once again. However, it remained silent for several more hours. Then suddenly, the tree spoke and gently said, "Have you been looking for me?" "Yes! Yes, I have", cried Liv. "Why am I here Dear Sage? How did you get from my parents' house to India of all places?" "I have always been with you but now I am dying", said the Wise Sage. "What do you mean you are dying", asked Liv. "We Oaks live very long lives my dear, but even we find a time to depart." "Not now!" Shouted Liv. "You can't leave me now. Whatever will I do without you?" cried Liv. The Wise Sage replied, "You will continue to unbecome." "Unbecome?" Questioned Liv. "Is that what this journey has been about? What do you mean to unbecome?" "This is your unbecoming my dear. A journey you had to go through to unlearn, surrender, and release all that was clouding your vision" commented Wise Old Sage. "My vision?" questioned Liv.

The Wise Sage went on to tell Liv about all of the times she lost her way. Whether she lost sight of her divine essence and her power to help others or listened to the words of those who truly could not speak of her purpose, the journey was to let it all go and recognize the true essence of her beauty from when she was created. "You have faced many challenges over the years, and met each guide with grace and certainty. You have defeated the three enemies and looked yourself in the eyes and saw God. This is your unbecoming." Liv felt an immense release as though decades of life had just shed from her being. She stopped and looked at the Wise Sage and asked what was next? "What does one do after unbecoming? What is left?" asked Liv. "It took you seeing nothing to see that you were already everything", said the Wise Sage. "Now just be," he commented. Liv asked "what will happen to you?" The Wise Sage replied, "Don't worry about me my dear. I will always be with you. Just look within whenever you need me."

Just then Liv felt the earth move under her feet. She thought for certain she was being taken home as she felt the journey was near complete. But just as she looked up to the sky, she noticed the tree was beginning to die. "NO!!!" she screamed. "You cannot go! I didn't go through all of this to lose you too!" Wise Old Sage just smiled as he began to harden. Liv laid her head at the base of the tree and didn't move, weeping with very little air returning to her lungs. She was exhausted. She felt she had lost it all. What was left? What was she to do?

After crying for several minutes, Liv lifted her head and caught her breath. She stood to her feet and began moving around the tree. She reached her hand out to touch the Wise Sage and suddenly felt a warm embrace. It was as if she was being hugged by many arms all at once. She felt the most incredible love she ever could imagine. Then suddenly, a voice spoke to Liv. "How many times have you touched the tree?" asked the voice. In that moment, Liv felt a renewed sense of why she had found herself in India. A land with everything and nothing. A place that felt more like home than any other place she had ever been before. "You can leave India whenever you want but trust that India will never leave you", said the man. "There is some kind of peace in all of the chaos that stays. It just gets to you. The love that every smile carries. The warmth of every face." Liv almost fell to the ground.

She noticed an uncanny similarity in the voice. "How…how are you talking to me?" said Liv. "Wise Old Oak I thought you left me" cried Liv. "I never left you my dear." And to her amazement, she commented, "You were the voice I heard in the cave." Liv felt a warm, gentle touch on her shoulder. She reached to touch the hand and turned around quickly. Liv remembered feeling her Dad's hand on her shoulder several times over the course of these journeys. Could this be him?

Liv jumped to her feet and saw a man standing before her. The man spoke and said, "I am not moving my love. I have been waiting for you." "How in the world are you here?" Asked Liv. "I thought you were my Dad." "I am sorry my dear. I know how much you miss him and he is always with you" commented the man. "But, how are you here now?" Liv cried. I have told you every story, every heart ache, every celebration in my life. Every day I couldn't wait to see you when I was a little girl, and I was shocked to find out you were here in India. What is going on? How are you here?" Liv touched the man seeing if he was real. He was beautiful. Eyes of caramel brown which seemed to twinkle in the star-lit night, long wavy hair with just a slight marking of silver to indicate his wisdom, and the softest touch you could ever imagine.

"I have been in you my dear. Waiting this entire time." Liv replied, "Waiting for what?" "You to find yourself my love. You were never lost. You simply thought you were. I have never moved." "But what about the tree?" Liv said with tears in her eyes. "Honestly, this was the first time I ever truly touched the tree. I was afraid that if I touched the tree I would somehow transfer my negative energy into it." The man gently put his finger to Liv's mouth and said "SHUSH. Life to life…being to being. They see everything if you just stand still. The tree may look hard from the outside but trust inside it is still soft and divine. Every groove, bend of the branch is meant for flexibility. Being there and being nothing" said the Man.

Liv immediately began to have flashes back to her childhood and all of the dreams and wishes she had as a little girl. She remembered everything but didn't feel an ounce of pain. What is happening? She asked the man. "The tree is not gone, replied the man. The tree is living as it lives in every breath as it symbolizes the tree of life. It never dies. It is always there. When you spoke to the tree, you spoke to a part of your own self which you were afraid to see. That part was me. I am you my love. The Wise Old Oak was nothing but a mere representation of yourself. Now you recognize all that you are. I arrive as a part of you. What part do I stand for? What are "we"? We are like two bodies having the same soul. Having the same purpose. We have been walking on the same path. As the roots are high above. The branches are the reality. You were in the branches my love. I was nowhere to be seen or to be found until you recognized yourself for what you truly are. I am a mirror reflection of your own higher self. I have been taking care of our soul and you have been taking care of our being. You are loved my dear. I have loved you from the moment we were created. I always knew you would find me." Just then, the Man lifted his hands and Liv's eyes opened wider than one could ever imagine. Before her were the two lanterns representing her children. The man touched her cheek softly, looked into her blue eyes, and said, "Welcome home my love, we have been waiting for you."

AFTERWORD

∞

So what happens for Liv and the man? Is this the man her father, Robert had told her about when she was a little girl? Or is this her divine masculine facing her once and for all? The second book in the series will highlight the time Liv spends in India. What role will the Man play in her continued spiritual growth? What about the kids? Will they be born in Book 2? The second book in this series will be released late Fall of 2019 so stay tuned. Come join Liv for her magical journey and see what awaits her on her next adventure.

Acknowledgments

∞

This book began in my busy mind well over a year ago. I tried to sit down and write, but the situation just never seemed to lend itself to the culmination of the final project. That was until this year. Then in one quick lift of the pen, the words just poured out onto the page and *The Unbecoming* breathed its first breath out into the Universe and was officially born.

First and foremost, thank you to my writing coach, best friend, and twin Gaurav Sehgal who made me look into my very own figurative reflective mirror and see my divine essence as a writer. Thank you for writing the beautiful poems specifically for *The Unbecoming* and for helping me find the words when the well ran dry. You are a beautiful soul.

To my children, Aleks and Olivia. The beautiful lanterns who show up each day and remind me to be present, to love with all my soul, and to never give up no matter what life serves me. I marvel in your beauty and ability to feel vs. think. Thank you for understanding when Mommy had to write, but also for forcing me out of the cave when the moments with family were far more important than the pen. To the sweet Bunny who sat by my side and never complained. Love you Bun Bun.

To Kent. Thank you for the support you showed me throughout the writing of this book. I know the dedication it takes to raise the God and Goddess we have as children and I am forever indebted to you.

Thank you to my Mother and Father. The stories in the novel represent many aspects of my own unbecoming. My parents laid a foundation of love and dedication despite the illusion of separation at times and always were there for me no matter the darkness that was present. My Mother is the Sun and my Father the moon.

To those who inspired the story of the guides, thank you for the presence in my life. You are the angels who I look to each day and who inspire me to keep going. Without you there would be no story. I am forever grateful to your presence in my life.

Last, but certainly not least, thank you to my devoted Instagram followers for the encouraging words and understanding when I went on my hiatus to write. You never left my side and remained lovingly loyal to the craft. I love you all to the Moon and back.

LIST OF CHARACTERS & SYMBOLS

∞

Liv

Liv is a precocious, introverted child who suffers tremendous anxiety. She is bullied by girls and boys over the course of her young schools days which leads her to find her safest place and most enjoyable time with her Dad, Robert. Liv is faced with several journeys over the course of her life, led by key guides who have been with her all of her life yet appear to her at various points in time. The guides aid Liv in finding her true inner beauty and strength to overcome several traumatic life events including the loss of her father, depression, the lacking relationship with her mother, cancer, and her own battle with self-limiting beliefs.

Dad (Robert)

Robert is Liv's Father. He is her hero and protector over the course of her life. Robert is a lover of history and reading and inspires Liv to go on and become an excellent student and Professor. Robert passes away from his battle with cancer which leads Liv into the shadow of despair. However, Robert will make a special appearance in several places throughout the book so pay attention closely to see the continued love and connection appear time and time again.

Wise Old Oak

Originally, the oak tree in her parent's yard, Liv has many talks with the tree over the course of her life. He is the keeper of her secrets, and the roots of her soul. Wise Old Oak knows everything about Liv and accepts her as she truly is. They share many beautiful moments under the stars. Wise Old Oak appears again in Ch. 5 when Liv arrives in India. How is he in India, she wonders. Wise Old Oak is dying and spends a very special moment with Liv. He is quintessential in her unbecoming and is a significant character throughout several chapters. How can he be in multiple places at the same time?

Mother (Anna)

Liv always had a distant relationship with her Mother, Anna. Ann grew up under the thumb of an overprotective Mother (Liv's Grandmother) who seemingly neglected Anna's emotional needs. Anna faced abuse as a young girl but yearned to break out of the control which caused her immense anxiety and fear. Anna represents the quintessential transition for Liv to truly align with her divine feminine.

Lucina

Lucina is the Goddess of Light. Lucina aids those who are vulnerable and shows them the light of hope in their darkest hours. Lucina meets Liv while in the darkest shadow of helplessness and despair as Liv contemplates ending her life. Lucina illuminates Liv's future and assists her on her journey in Iceland. It is Lucina who presents Liv with Freya's sword and clarifies Liv's free will in choosing battle or love and compassion. She is also the key to Liv aligning with herself as the Mother of All.

Freya's Sword

Freya, twin brother of Freyr, is the Goddess of love, beauty, fertility and war. Her brother Freyr is said to have went into battle forgetting his sword which resulted in his death. Freya began to struggle with the duality of her existence and is said to have chosen to focus on her gift of love and beauty vs. fighting in battle. Liv's Mother Anna read her many stories of the beautiful Freya as a child and grew up emulating the warrior aspect of Freya. The sword is evident in several locations in the story and is pivotal in the union of Liv's divine feminine and masculine energies.

Little Anna

Within the story, Liv's will travel to Iceland to face her mother, Little Anna at the age of seven. Little Anna has been physically abused by an elder man in town. Liv becomes enraged and goes to confront the man. Little Anna and Liv spend time under the stars just as Liv and her Dad once did. They develop a special bond, in which Liv becomes a surrogate Mother for Liv and provides her with the emotional support and protection that she needs. Little Anna experiences a great shift in Ch. 3.

The Shoe Maker

The shoe maker is the man who is physically abusing Little Anna. He makes an appearance in Ch. 3 while Liv is in Iceland. Distraught at the sight of Little Anna's bruises, Liv takes Freya's sword and storms into town to teach the shoe maker the ultimate lesson. You don't mess around with her Mother and live to tell the tale. You don't want to miss this epic battle in Ch. 3. This is the free will Lucina presents to Liv as she aligns with her divine feminine.

The Destroyer

A major guide in Liv's journey to the unbecoming. He is the Father of Creation and the guide of the lost souls. As the Destroyer of illusion, he guides Liv to face her greatest battle...that battle of her own inability to see her true inner self and divine power. The Destroyer has a father presence about him that Liv finds great comfort in. He doesn't take Liv's insecurities lightly and demands she looks herself in a reflective mirror within the cave. Don't miss what comes of Liv in Ch. 4 as she truly yearns to unbecome.

The Reflective Mirror

The reflective mirror represents Liv's internal realization of the self as divine. She begins to see her true self without scars or external influences. She sees the purest form of her soul in this moment with the guidance of the Destroyer.

Raj

Raj is a kind cab driver who finds Liv in India. He is summoned by a voice to find her in the park. He refuses to leave her side and helps her find her way. He recognizes the Wise Old Oak from Liv's phone and takes her to the tree. Raj is a kind face in a foreign land, but Liv quickly learns that India truly is her home.

The Man in India

The most endearing character of the story. The man presents himself to Liv at many points throughout the story. But it isn't until she defeats the three enemies in Ch. 4 that he manifests before her in Ch. 5. He represents the spirit of the divine masculine which is present throughout many aspects of the story. When he manifests before her, Liv is stunned. She recognizes many similarities of his character and voice as she has seen him or heard him before. Find out who this mysterious man is in Ch. 5. Could this be the man Liv's father always told her about when she was a little girl? Or is this another part of her identity yearning to be found?

ABOUT THE AUTHOR

∞

Dr. Renee is an Educational Psychologist, Associate Professor of Educational Psychology and owner of Transcendent Heart Life Coaching. Dr. Renee is a leading researcher and expert in emotion regulation, management, and recovery after trauma. She has published articles in the area of teacher emotion regulation and emotional development of children and adults.

As a young child and adolescent, Dr. Renee faced many sleepless nights and days living in fear of when the next panic attack would come. She grew up thinking life was scary and unpredictable. She spent most of her 20s worrying about all the things that could go wrong in her life only to find she wasn't living at all. In fact, it was only in to her 30s that she truly began to listen to her inner "voice" when facing a monumental turning point after facing a major life/health issue. It was this turning point that forced her to decide who she was and what she was capable of.

Despite having a Ph.D. in the field of educational psychology and two decades of teaching experience, Dr. Renee knew there was still so much more learn. It was after this journey that she found that she truly conquered the "enemies" of internal doubt, negative thinking, and hopelessness. She found her true purpose and the most amazing sense of bliss one could ever imagine. She learned the principles of emotional authenticity and how to implement these into her everyday life to show up and be fully present.

Dr. Renee became a better mother and partner through her own unbecoming. She also improved her career potential and began an amazing program helping many move out of the emotional trauma and into meaningful and loving relationships that one can find peace within. Young children are also benefitting from her programs in which she helps tweens and teens cultivate self-love and move into a space of self-empowerment. Visit Dr. Renee's website www.transcendentheart.com for further information.

About the Book

∞

The Unbecoming is science-fiction/fantasy tale of the journey of a young woman, Liv as she ventures throughout time to unbecome all that she thought she was destined to be. Liv awakens after the loss of her father only to find that she does not even recognize herself. Who has she become? Why does she continue to struggle and choose the challenging ways of life? Can she be anything else or is this her plight? Liv is met throughout the story by five key guides who essentially show her the way to self-actualization, however, it doesn't come as she imagined. This is an emotional tale of unlearning, surrendering, and letting go…the ultimate journey to the Unbecoming.